Ruby the Red Fairy

Choose your own Magic

by Daisy Meadows

ORCHARD BOOKS

www.rainbowmagic.co.uk

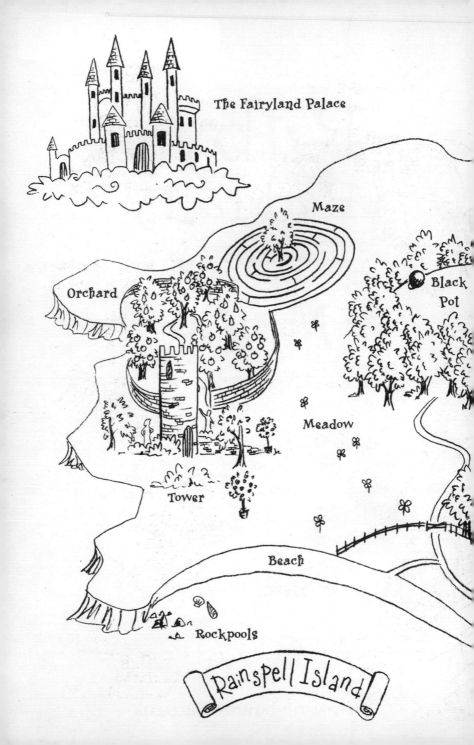

Special thanks to Mandy Archer.

For Ruby Flew,
with love and fairy wishes x

HIT entertainment

A CIP catalogue record for this book is available
from the British Library.

ISBN 978 1 40830 789 2
1 3 5 7 9 10 8 6 4 2

Printed in Great Britain

The paper and board used in this paperback are natural recyclable
products made from wood grown in sustainable forests. The
manufacturing processes conform to the environmental regulations
of the country of origin.

Orchard Books is a division of Hachette Children's Books,

an Hachette UK company

www.hachette.co.uk

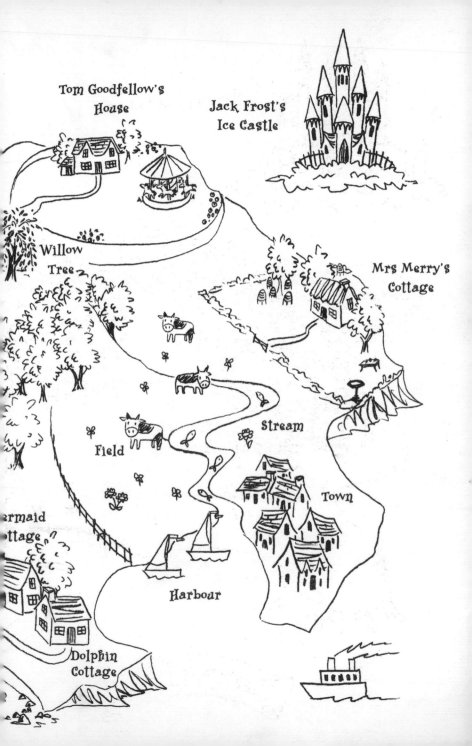

There's no place for me in Fairyland,
A land of smiles and fun,
My goblins will not roam there,
I loathe its golden sun!

Now I hear there's a new helper,
Someone good and true,
A friend of Rainbow Magic,
A person just like you...

I'll hide a pretty fairy,
And set a tricky quest.
Can you find the precious Ruby,
And foil my cruellest test?

Ruby the Red Fairy
needs your help!

Can you be the special friend
who helps Ruby in her time of need...?
All you have to do is believe in magic,
open the pages of this book and choose
your own path through the story to rescue
Ruby from wicked Jack Frost! There
are lots of different routes you can
take and plenty of fairy friends to
help you along the way!

1

It's the start of the weekend and you're in your bedroom, listening to music.

As you dance in front of the mirror, something catches your eye. A cascade of fuchsia glitter reveals a pretty fairy with shiny brown bunches!

"Hello!" she says, her voice tinkling like a miniature bell. "My name is Sienna the Saturday Fairy."

You gasp as Sienna points her tiny pink wand at the mirror in front of you. Suddenly it transforms into a magic looking glass – it's misty at first but it then clears to reveal the rooftops of Fairyland.

"Why are the toadstools so pale?" you ask, pointing to the faded fairy houses dotted over the hillside.

"They used to be bright red," says Sienna, and then her face falls. "But now they've lost their colour."

You lead your new friend over to the windowsill, then take a seat on the bed. Sienna smooths out

★ Turn to the next page! ★

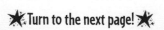

her skirt and tells you that Jack Frost has
kidnapped Ruby the Red Fairy! The mean Ice
Lord has been plotting a scheme like this ever
since Ruby forgot to invite him to the Midsummer
Ball. The Rainbow Fairies and all their friends
have searched Fairyland from top to bottom,
but she has disappeared.

"Ruby must be somewhere in the human
world," adds Sienna. "That's why I decided to
find you."

The little fairy flutters over to touch your hand.
"We know you've got a kind heart and that you
believe in magic. Can you help find Ruby and
bring the red back to Fairyland?"

You smile and nod your head at once.

"Thank you so much!" Sienna claps her hands,
her little wings trembling with excitement. "There's
not a moment a lose!"

* If you decide to peer into the looking glass to see if you can
  spot anything, go to 9.
* If you decide to start your search in Fairyland, go to 33.

You flap your wings as hard as you can, setting your sights on the Fairyland Palace. Although it is strange to be flying without Sienna to guide you, the sunshine feels warm on your wings and they seem to know which way to go.

"That must be it!" you cry out loud, as the palace's magnificent pink turrets loom into view. Instead of landing, however, something urges you to press on. You flutter further and further through the clouds until you grow tired.

When you finally drop down from the sky, you find yourself in a pretty garden where a human girl is playing with a cat.

"I'm back in the human world!" you gasp.

The girl looks up and smiles. "Yes, you're in Wetherbury!" she grins. "Are you a Rainbow Magic Fairy?"

"I'm a friend of the fairies," you nod shyly, fluttering down to rest on an upturned flowerpot.

"Me too!" beams the girl. "My name is Kirsty Tate."

⭐ Turn to the next page! ⭐

Kirsty leads you indoors, where another girl with curly blonde hair is reading a book. The girl's face lights up the minute she sees you.

"What a lovely surprise!" she says in a friendly voice. "I'm Rachel, Kirsty's best friend."

You take a seat on Kirsty's dressing table. After you've explained everything, the girls give you a precious piece of advice.

"If Ruby is with Jack Frost's goblins," warns Kirsty, "there's bound to be all kinds of trouble."

Rachel nods her head and shudders. "Goblins can't help getting into scrapes and mishaps! So when you find trouble, Ruby won't be far away."

You thank the girls, and tell them that you must hurry away to press on with the search.

* **If you decide to take a right towards Wetherbury Village Hall, go to 11.**
* **If you would rather fly on towards the high street, go to 27.**

You flutter into the sunshine, desperate to find Ruby before Jack Frost and his goblins cause complete chaos!

As the afternoon draws on, you begin to worry. What if you can't find Ruby before bedtime? You can't bear to think of the poor little fairy alone in the dark, far away from home.

A swallow curves past you, gliding in elegant loops. You follow the bird for a moment or two, before gasping in amazement. The sky before you is lit up by a stunning sunset glowing in golds, crimsons and pinks.

This is the first time you've seen anything red all day – could it be a sign from Ruby? You clasp the rose necklace and wish as hard as you can.

"I don't know any spells," you begin. "But I do believe in magic."

Red fairy dust suddenly sparkles from Ruby's jewelled rose, covering you in a mist of glitter.

When the mist clears you find yourself standing where the sunset meets the land, outside Wetherbury Village Hall. Before you can collect yourself, a fairy darts out of the hall, clasps your hand and drags you back inside.

"Hurry, hurry!" she whispers. "Come with me!"

The pretty fairy has glossy black hair, held

★ Turn to the next page! ★

in place with a scarlet rose. Her frilled skirt is hemmed with eye-catching orange ruffles.

She looks over her shoulder and smiles. "I'm Saskia the Salsa Fairy, by the way."

"Come back here!" bellows an angry voice.

A mob of green goblins stomp after you. It's not hard to see that they are all hopping mad.

"I came here to peep at the village dance class," explains the Dance Fairy. "But I think I interrupted some goblin mischief."

You take another long look at Saskia's deep-red dance outfit, your eyes glistening with excitement. If Saskia's clothes have still got their lovely shades of red, could Ruby be hidden somewhere near?

* If you decide to dart around the hall searching for Ruby, go to 5.

* If you choose to tiptoe round the back of the hall so you can hatch a plan, go to 40.

4

You fly away in search of Ruby, wondering if you can escape through the door marked 'Kitchen'. When you venture into the kitchen, you can't believe the mess and muddle that the goblins have created! The two greedy creatures have eaten nearly all the pastries from the café.

You are tiptoeing past a box of faded jammy doughnuts when a tiny voice calls out to you.

"Pssst! Over here!"

You look up to see Scarlett the Garnet Fairy, waving from behind a bag of flour on a shelf. Scarlett's face is full of smiles, but her frilly dress has faded so much that you can almost see right through her!

You flutter up and hide together on the shelf.

"Can you use your magic to stop the goblins from causing mischief?" you ask.

Scarlett shakes her head sadly. "I'm trapped here. Without the intense scarlet of my gemstone, my powers are far too weak," she explains.

* If you think that Ruby's rose necklace might give you the magic you need, go to 20.
* If you think you'll have more luck pushing the bag of flour onto the goblins' heads, go to 26.

"Let's look around the hall!" you urge Saskia. "Ruby must be trapped somewhere."

Saskia flits left and right, ducking each time the naughty creatures swipe at her with their fists.

"We've got to find Ruby soon," she cries. "My wings are getting tired!"

As you look at the mob of goblins, you notice that one of them is clutching a jar, and you see that Ruby is trapped inside!

"We'll have to trick them into letting Ruby go!" you whisper to Saskia.

You flutter behind the goblin holding the jar and shout into his ear. Your fairy-sized voice is light and tinkly, but you get the goblin's attention.

"What silly oafs you all are! You can't even catch two tiny fairies!" you tease them.

Then Saskia clicks her heels together and performs a whirling salsa for the gaping goblin. "How clumsy you are!" she laughs.

As the angry goblin reaches to grab the Dance Fairy, the jar falls from his hand and smashes to the floor. Suddenly, the hall fills with a blaze of red and scarlet.

"At last!" beams Ruby, fluttering away from the remains of the jar. "I'm free!"

* If you decide to return Ruby to the Fairyland Palace straightaway, go to 23.
* If you decide to get rid of the goblins for good, go to 41.

With a wave of Ruby's wand, you find yourselves
sliding down a rainbow. The colourful arch curves
through the clouds, before dipping down into the
stunning hillsides of Fairyland.

"Look!" you call to Ruby. "All the reds have
come back into the toadstools!"

Ruby grins as she lands on the grass. "It's time
to go up to the Fairyland Palace," she says.

You feel your heart leap with excitement.

"Please take your necklace back first," you
tell her. You take it off and hand it to her.

Ruby gives you a big hug. "That belongs to
you now," she smiles. "Please keep it as a token of
my thanks."

She slips the necklace back over your head.
Suddenly, scarlet stars surround Ruby
and another pendant appears
on her neck. The rose
looks just as beautiful
as yours.

"Now we will
be linked forever,"
she laughs. "True
fairy friends!"

The End

You flutter up to a shelf and hide behind a rolling pin so that you can overhear what the goblins are talking about. It seems that the naughty pair are delighted with their mischief!

"We've caused all kinds of trouble since Jack Frost snatched that horrible fairy," chuckles one of them.

You hope that the wicked creatures might give you a clue about where Ruby is, but instead they just talk about all the food they've stolen. It's only when they've eaten their fourth doughnut that one of them grimaces.

"This faded jam isn't half as tasty as the real red stuff," he grumbles, rubbing his tummy.

You creep forward for a closer look, but accidentally send the rolling pin spinning off the shelf.

"Ouch!"

You look over the edge and tremble. The rolling pin has landed on the goblin's head with a bump!

* **If you flutter out of the back door before the goblins can see you, go to 34.**

* **If you decide to squeeze yourself through a crack in the window, go to 25.**

You glide up towards the rainbow. As you flutter along the arch you count the colours, but realise that there are only six! You sigh and press on, sad to think of a rainbow without Ruby's dazzling blaze of red.

Before long, the rainbow begins to dip back down through the clouds, arching towards a glinting stretch of ocean. You follow the bow until it touches the ground in a forest clearing.

"What's that?" you wonder, pointing to an old black cooking pot turned on its side.

"Hello!" says a friendly voice. You turn to see two girls bounding towards you.

"Am I in the human world?" you ask shyly, landing softly on the blackened pot.

★ Turn to the next page! ★

"Yes," replies the girl with long brown hair. "This is Rainspell Island."

"My name is Rachel Walker," says the blonde girl. "And this is my best friend, Kirsty Tate."

"We're old friends of the Rainbow Magic fairies," beams Kirsty. "Which one are you?"

You take a deep breath and explain everything.

"See that old black pot?" Kirsty says when you've finished. "That's where poor Ruby was trapped when we first met her!"

"I'm so cross that Jack Frost is up his old tricks again," frowns Rachel.

"Do you know where I can find Ruby?" you ask hopefully.

The friends both shake their heads sadly.

Kirsty looks thoughtful. "Keep a look out for goblins," she says.

"Yes, if you can find the goblins," smiles Rachel, "Ruby won't be far away."

You thank the girls, then get ready to go goblin-hunting!

* If you decide to flutter past the cottage up ahead, go to 17.

* If you'd rather follow the stream down towards the harbour, go to 56.

You step forward to peer into the magical mirror in front of you, Sienna fluttering at your shoulder.

"Without Ruby the Red Fairy, our kingdom has become dull and drab," she sighs. The tiny fairy touches the glass with her wand and a new picture forms.

"Isn't that King Oberon and Queen Titania?" you ask.

The mirror shows the king and queen inside the Fairyland Palace. Without its rich red velvet carpets and curtains, the room looks faded and grey. Sienna points to six fairies sitting quietly in the corner.

"There's Amber, Saffron, Fern, Sky, Izzy and Heather!" she explains. "They look so sad without their sister."

Sienna taps the mirror one last time. Suddenly the glass is filled with a picture of Jack Frost in his Ice Castle. He's sitting on his throne and

⭐ Turn to the next page! ⭐

laughing menacingly. Behind him you can see
a couple of his goblin servants.

"That horrid creature has got to be stopped!"
you cry. "Poor Ruby!"

"Believe in the power of good and you can't
fail," smiles Sienna. "Are you ready for some
magic?"

* **If you decide to reach out and hold Sienna in your hand, go to 21.**

* **If you choose to close your eyes and imagine where Ruby might be, go to 32.**

"We have to find Ruby before the goblins take her too far away," you decide. "Let's go now!"

The Rainbow Fairies all nod in agreement.

But Sienna asks, "Are you brave enough to go on the search alone? If we leave Fairyland, Jack Frost might cause even more trouble."

"I-I think so," you reply. "But where do I start?"

"Your heart will lead you in the right direction," Amber the Orange Fairy tells you.

You flutter your wings and make your way towards the rainbow that stretches across the sky. As you wave goodbye to Sienna and the Rainbow Fairies, something shiny catches your eye. You glide back and pick up a red rose pendant from the grass. The necklace glints in the light, sending scarlet beams all around.

"That's Ruby's favourite necklace!" cries Amber.

Sienna the Saturday Fairy carefully puts the necklace over your head. "You must take this with you," she says. "It's still glowing with Ruby's magic."

The fairies join hands and form a ring to wish you good luck. As you glide skywards, you can just make out their voices singing over the trees. "Good luck! And remember – follow your heart!"

* If you decide to head towards the Fairyland Palace, go to 2.

* If you think it's best to flutter up towards the rainbow that you've spotted in the sky above you, go to 8.

11

You wave goodbye and smile as you flutter down the country lane outside Kirsty's house, towards Wetherbury Village Hall.

Honk, honk!

As you flutter just above the trees, you're surprised to see a line of cars trailing right back to the village. The people inside them look very angry! You fly down to find out what is causing the hold-up.

"Mind out!" shouts one driver.

"It's my turn!" bellows another.

Up ahead is a set of traffic lights, but they are all stuck on green! Without a red light, all the cars are trying to move at once, and this is blocking the road.

In the middle of the road a policeman is blowing his whistle and waving his arms around so furiously that it's causing even more confusion!

You dart forwards to take a closer look.

"That's no policeman!" you gasp. "It's a goblin dressed up in a policeman's outfit!"

If there are goblins causing trouble in Wetherbury, perhaps Ruby is nearby?

"She must be locked under a powerful spell if the red is disappearing here too," you whisper.

Suddenly the goblin blows his whistle and looks up, spotting you.

"Oi!" he thunders, shaking his fist at you. "Come here!"

The goblin starts running towards you, his hat tumbling onto the road.

You look for help, but all you can see is a queue of cross drivers and a mum pushing her baby along the pavement in a buggy.

* If you try to hide in the baby's buggy, go to 31.

* If you decide to flutter over the goblin's head instead, go to 48.

You chase after the goblins as fast your wings can
carry you, wondering where they might be going
in such a rush. At last, you pass a sign that says
Wetherbury Village.

While you decide where to go next, you look
up to see a kite dipping and turning in the skies.

You gasp when you see that it is a stunning
shade of red! Your heart gives a little leap. Surely
Ruby must be close by?

You flutter on towards the kite. As you get closer,
you see that it is being flown by some children
who are sharing a picnic. And there, hiding behind
a bush, are the greedy goblins! They're licking

their lips at the sight of all that food.

Suddenly a tiny flash of light weaves in and out of the picnic feast.

"Could that be Ruby?" you say out loud.

A little fairy with stripy tights flits over to you.

"I'm afraid not," she smiles. "I'm Cherry the Cake Fairy."

Cherry takes your hand and leads you behind some flowers. "I'm sure that Ruby is very close!" Cherry declares. "We've just got to find her."

* **If you suggest that Cherry teases the goblins while you take a closer look around, go to 16.**

* **If you decide to trick the goblins into telling you where Ruby is, go to 19.**

You give Ruby a hug. While the goblins squabble about which one of them is going to confess to Jack Frost, you and Ruby prepare to return to Fairyland!

"There's a dance class in the hall tonight," grins Saskia. "I'm going to stay and enjoy the music!"

You and Ruby give Saskia a farewell hug, then fly hand-in-hand through the melting red sunset.

"You have been a true and brave fairy friend," smiles Ruby, slipping her rose necklace back over her golden plaits.

"It's been magical," you reply, as you approach the hillsides of Fairyland. It's lovely to see that the colour has returned to the toadstool houses, and they are a bright cherry-red once more.

"Oh, look!" cries Ruby all of a sudden.

Amber, Saffron, Fern, Sky, Izzy and Heather are fluttering towards you, their arms outstretched to welcome you and Ruby home!

The End

You fly higher and higher until the ground beneath you disappears from sight. Soon, the clouds part to reveal the patchwork fields of Wetherbury. You wonder if Ruby could be trapped somewhere in the meadows and hedgerows, but there isn't a fairy or even a goblin in sight.

As you make your way through the clouds, the afternoon sun begins to fade and sink in the sky.

"Oh, my goodness!" you cry out loud, dazzled by the beauty of the sunset.

The light sends sunbeams all over Wetherbury, covering the ground in russets, golds and reds. You fly towards it as fast as you can.

"If there is red in the sky," you smile, "surely Ruby must be nearby!"

You dart to the point where the sun touches the horizon, just above a village hall. You land gently on the rooftop, wondering what to do next.

You don't have to wonder for long – there's a huge commotion going on inside the hall. You flutter down to a ledge and peep in through a window.

"Pesky fairies!" bellows an ugly voice. "We'll trap you, too!"

You jump back in fright at the sight of a crowd

of angry goblins. Up above their heads, a tiny
fairy is darting left and right. You have to strain
your ears to hear her over the din.

"I'm Saskia the Salsa Fairy," she cries.
"And you're too slow to catch me!"

The fairy stamps her feet and shakes her
skirts at the naughty creatures. You're relieved to
see that her frilly costume dazzles in a stunning
deep scarlet.

"Ruby must be nearby!" you squeak excitedly.

* If you decide to try and find Ruby in the hall, go
  to 5.

* If you think it's wiser to fly up to Saskia and offer your
  help, go to 28.

You ask Sienna to take you to the Rainbow Fairies.

"Follow me," she nods, pointing down to a beautiful woodland grove.

You land near a flowerbed. You spot poppies, lilies and pansies. The blooms are faded, but still slightly dappled with red – could Ruby be near?

"Hello!" cries a sweet voice. It's not Ruby...it's Izzy the Indigo Fairy! She flutters out to greet you, followed by Amber, Saffron, Fern, and Heather.

"It's lovely to meet you," you say politely.

A hand gently touches your shoulder. You spin round to see Sky the Blue Fairy hovering beside you.

"We're so thrilled you came," she whispers, giving you a hug.

"We were picking flowers here with Ruby when she disappeared," explains Amber.

* If you decide to carry on with your search, go to 10.

* If you think it's better to stay and explore the grove, go to 18.

"You distract the goblins," you whisper to Cherry. "I'll see if I can find Ruby."

Bravely, Cherry flies towards the goblins.

The goblins stomp after the fairy, swiping at her with clumpy green fists. But the Party Fairy distracts them with little red cherries that burst from her wand with a tantalising *pop!*

While they stumble across the field, you search for Ruby. Where can she be?

Just when you're about to give up, the rose pendant starts to sparkle. Tiny glittering stars bounce through the air and land on a pretty rose bush.

You flutter over, your wings trembling with excitement. In the centre of one of the dark red roses is Ruby, trapped by an icy set of thorns.

"Don't worry, Ruby!" you cry.

You delicately touch each thorn with the rose pendant. In an instant the sharp prickles melt and disappear.

The Red Fairy shakes her golden hair, red stars fizzing all around her.

"You saved me!" she beams. "Thank you so much!"

* If you decide to take Ruby straight back to Fairyland, go to 6.

* If you choose to help Ruby return her reds to the human world, go to 30.

17

You fly across the Rainspell countryside, with the girls' words ringing in your ears. As you flutter across the hedgerows, you soon see an old lady in her cottage garden, tending her beehives. You study the garden closely, but not a leaf is out of place – the goblins can't have been here today.

At last you approach the quaint town on Rainspell. You zigzag in and out of the crowds, taking care to hide yourself from the shoppers and holidaymakers.

Just then you hear a loud shout coming from a café.

"Where's my tea?" bellows a man. "I've been waiting here for ages."

You peer through the window and spot a queue of unhappy people shouting at the café owner.

"I don't think I can eat this strawberry sundae," says one little boy to his mum.

You dart inside and peer over his shoulder. On the table is a dismal-looking dessert melting away in pale shades of pink and grey.

You glance at the tables around you – none of the food looks quite right in this café! A man is staring at a plate of fish and chips topped off with a big squirt of grey paste that is meant to be

★ Turn to the next page! ★

tomato ketchup. It seems that anything red has completely disappeared!

You gasp and shake your head, guessing that this is the sort of trouble Kirsty and Rachel warned you about! You flutter to the back of the café and see two naughty goblins chuckling as they stuff jammy doughnuts into their mouths.

So where can Ruby be? you wonder. The poor Fairy must be trapped by a dreadfully powerful spell if all the red is seeping away from Rainspell Island, too.

* If you decide to flutter away in search of the missing fairy, go to 4.

* If you choose to confront the goblins, go to 45.

You take Fern's hand and ask her to show you around the grove. Suddenly, something sparkly catches your eye. You stoop down to pick up a fairy necklace that is lying on the grass.

"That's Ruby's rose pendant!" cries Fern. She calls to Sienna and her Rainbow sisters.

Saffron touches the delicate chain. "It must have fallen off when she disappeared. That explains why there are still touches of red on some of the flowers here!"

As Saffron holds the pendant close to her heart, the necklace releases a small ripple of scarlet stars.

"You must take this with you," she tells you. "There is still a little of Ruby's magic inside."

You reach for Sienna's hand, but the fairy smiles and steps back. "Jack Frost is determined to cause trouble here," she explains. "We need to stay and defend Fairyland. Can you find Ruby on your own?"

You nod, as all the fairies flutter round for a farewell hug. "Goodbye and good luck!"

* If you decide to head north towards the pink towers of the Fairyland Palace, go to 2.

* If you choose to fly south towards the Rainbow Fairies' toadstool village, go to 39.

You and Cherry work out a plan, then flutter over to the goblins' hiding place in the hedgerow.

"Are you two hungry?" you call.

The goblins tumble out of the hedgerow, rubbing their tummies hungrily. Cherry waves her wand, sending cascades of fairy dust spiralling into the sky. Suddenly, a scrummy-looking chocolate cake appears.

The greedy pair swipe at the cake, but it's too high for them to reach.

"You can have all of this," you announce, "if you tell us where Ruby is hidden."

"No way!" says one goblin.

The other goblin sighs. "We aren't allowed to tell you about the tree over there!"

You and Cherry immediately flutter towards the tree as fast as your wings can carry you.

"There's Ruby!" you cry. "She's trapped by a layer of ice!"

Suddenly, her necklace, which you are holding, begins to glow brightly, melting the ice to nothing.

"Thank you so much!" cries Ruby happily.

* If you decide to help Ruby put the reds back all over the world, go to 30.

* If you choose to use Ruby's magic to escape back to Fairyland, go to 51.

You look at Scarlett and frown — these naughty goblins need to be stopped before they cause any more trouble!

You touch Ruby's necklace and feel it glow around your neck. You quickly reach out for Scarlett's hands. A little flurry of magic fizzes out of the necklace, landing on a pot of cutlery.

"Look!" you whisper. "They're flying by themselves!"

Scarlett giggles as the spoons jig through the air, before landing on the goblins. The panicked pair are given a series of little nudges and smacks as the utensils prod and poke them towards the back door.

"Hey!" squeals a goblin, dropping his doughnut. "Leave us alone!"

But within seconds the enchanted cutlery has driven the goblins out of the café!

"That's those two taken care of for now!" you grin. "I'd better carry on with my search for Ruby."

Scarlett flutters forwards to give you a big farewell hug.

"Good luck," she sings. "And be careful!"

* If you decide to flutter after the goblins, go to 12.

* If you think it's best if you float out of the door and upwards till they are out of sight, go to 14.

You reach out your hand and Sienna flutters over to stand on your palm.

"If you're going to help us," she says, "you're going to need to be able to fly."

The fairy waves her pink wand, her little star bracelet glinting in the light as a shower of tiny stars cascades onto your hair. Suddenly you have a funny shrinking feeling, before *pop!* – you're the same size as Sienna!

"I'm tiny!" you gasp.

Sienna laughs prettily. "Take a look at your back!"

You look behind you to see a beautiful pair of rainbow-coloured fairy wings. You twirl round and round, transfixed as the wings begin to flap. Gently your toes lift up, until you find yourself gliding in circles round your bedroom!

Sienna takes your hand and together you flutter towards the open window.

You take a deep breath and then push away from the window frame!

* If you choose to loop-the-loop until you've perfected your flying skills, go to 44.

* If you decide to fly as fast as you can towards Fairyland, go to 53.

The light zigs left, then right, before finally stopping to reveal a fairy! She has long auburn hair and a floaty orange dress.

She introduces herself as Erin the Firebird Fairy, and quickly leads you into the bushes.

Her beautiful firebird, Giggles, is perched in the brambles. But the bird isn't giggling happily like he should.

"Since the goblins arrived, Giggles' tail feathers have turned a dowdy shade of brown," sighs Erin. "Now the poor thing can't use his magic properly."

"Did his feathers used to be red?" you ask, reaching out to stroke the magical animal.

Erin nods. "Giggles has the power to spread humour, but without his fiery tail the whole town has fallen into a miserable mood."

"I bet Ruby is trapped somewhere nearby," you say. "As soon as I can free her, Giggles will get his colour and his magic back."

"Thank you," smiles Erin. "Good luck with finding Ruby!"

* If you decide to fly away to the right, go to 3.

* If you think you'll have more luck creeping out of the bushes and flying left, go to 14.

"Let's go to Fairyland," you suggest to Ruby.

Ruby's eyes light up. "Oh yes, I can't wait to see my sisters!"

"I'll make sure everything is back to normal in Wetherbury," says Saskia, giving you each a hug.

"Thank you," Ruby beams, as you slip the rose pendant over her golden hair.

Then, with a wave of her wand, you are back at the Fairyland Palace. King Oberon, Queen Titania and all the Rainbow Fairies rush forward to greet you. The king touches the ground with his royal sceptre and in an instant the room is decked in rich reds and scarlets, just as it ought to be.

"I should go," you sigh, thinking about your bedroom at home.

"Of course," agrees the queen. "But first, we want to show you something."

Ruby slips her little arm through yours, then leads you to the royal balcony. In the courtyard below are all of the Rainbow Magic fairies, clapping and cheering!

"The whole of Fairyland wants to say thank you for being so very brave!" smiles Ruby.

The End

You glimpse a red dot in the distance and set off after it. The shape is the first red thing you have spotted all day – what could it be?

As you get closer you see that the dot is actually a kite, dipping and circling in the afternoon sky.

You can't help feeling excited, but your heart flutters when you notice goblins trudging through the fields in the same direction. At last you get close enough to see who is flying the kite – a group of children about your age! The boys and girls are having a lovely time playing in the sunshine and enjoying a picnic tea. When you look at the yummy sticky buns and sandwiches, you realise that the greedy goblins are after all that delicious food!

All of a sudden, the kite dips and nearly crashes into you!

"Help!" you cry, somersaulting out of the way.

Suddenly the kite pulls up, almost inviting you to clamber on. It's as if someone is steering it from above!

You hold onto the kite to catch your breath, before spotting Cherry the Cake Fairy clinging to the kite's tail, her bunches blowing merrily in the breeze.

⭐ Turn to the next page! ⭐

"Climb up next to me!" she shouts.

You pull yourself up next to Cherry.

"I spotted the red kite, too," the little fairy explains. "I wondered if Ruby might be near."

You ride the kite together for a while, desperate to catch sight of the missing fairy.

* If you decide to get Cherry to divert the goblins' attention while you search for Ruby, go to 16.

* If you think it's better to use Ruby's necklace to summon the rest of the Rainbow Magic Fairies, go to 37.

Even at your tiny size it's quite a squeeze to push yourself out of the window, but somehow you manage it! You flutter out behind the café, before stopping to rest in a holly bush.

As you stop and turn, you see that the goblins have spotted you and are running to catch up. The first one reaches in to grab you, but he yelps as something hits him on the head!

You look up to see a fairy hurling berries down at the meanies. The berries aren't glossy red anymore, but they certainly manage to send the goblins on their way!

"Hello!" the fairy says, beaming proudly. "I'm Holly the Christmas Fairy. It's my job to put the sparkle into the festive season."

Suddenly Holly's face falls. Her eyes brim with tears as she explains that without Santa's red suit and Rudolph's red nose, Christmas isn't going to be fun this year!

"Don't worry, Holly!" you reply firmly. "I'll make things right again."

You hug farewell, then get on your way.

* **If you decide to fly away in the direction of the two naughty goblins, go to 12.**
* **If you'd rather flutter in the opposite direction, go to 24.**

Without Scarlett's magic, you decide to work together to push the big bag of flour onto the goblins' heads. It's a tricky job for two tiny fairies, but at last you manage to shove the flour to the edge.

"We can do it!" cheers Scarlett. "Heave!"

With one final push the flour is sent tumbling down, hiding the room in a cloud of white.

"Arghh!" yells a goblin, bumping into the other one. "What's happening?"

"I don't like it!" shouts the other. "Let's go!"

The cowards jump up and run panicking out of the back of the shop, bumping into each other as they go.

Scarlett flutters over to give you a high-five.

"We did it!" she beams. "Thank you so much."

You and Scarlett hug each other.

"I must go now," you say. "I need to find Ruby before those goblins stir up any more trouble!"

* If you decide to flutter out of the back door, go to 3.

* If you'd prefer to fly towards a tiny red dot that you can see bobbing in the distance, go to 24.

You wave goodbye to Kirsty and Rachel, then fly as fast you can, across the Tates' back garden, past the weather vane and towards the village high street.

Before you can get very far, however, you are greeted by the loud honking of car horns and the sound of people shouting. You flutter into the branch of a nearby tree, where a sweet grey squirrel is sitting.

"Hello, friend," you say. "What's going on?"

The little creature points to the street below. The winding road is crammed with a queue of cars and angry drivers.

A traffic jam here seems a little odd to you. You fly up to the traffic lights at the top of the road to take a closer look.

"That's why there's a jam!" you gasp. "Both sets of lights are fixed on green!"

Suddenly, you hear shouting.

"What's happened to my bucket?"

A workman who had been painting a yellow line down the side of the road is staring furiously at an

★ Turn to the next page! ★

upturned bucket of yellow paint!

You can't help but notice that someone has stamped big yellow footprints up and down the street…goblins!

"Goblin trouble must mean that Ruby is nearby," you whisper, keeping your fingers crossed.

Without a red traffic light, all the cars are trying to move at once and no one is getting anywhere!

As you dart above the chaos, you realise that Ruby must be trapped by a very powerful spell for all the red to have drained out of Wetherbury, too.

* If you choose to follow the yellow paint footprints that lead to the left, go to 38.

* If you decide to follow the yellow paint footprints that lead to the right, go to 52.

You fly into the village hall over the goblins' heads.

Saskia the Salsa Fairy smiles at you, then catches sight of your necklace. Quickly, she whispers a plan. You're going to trick the silly goblins into telling you where Ruby is!

"You're wearing Ruby's rose pendant," Saskia says, winking at you. "It has special magic powers."

"I want it!" roars one goblin.

The green meanies try to grab the pendant from you. But you easily manage to avoid them.

"Why do you want the necklace?" you ask, trying to sound confused. "The magic only works when Ruby the Red Fairy is nearby."

"Ruby's in the garden," a big-mouthed goblin blurts out.

You and Saskia immediately fly out to the village hall garden.

You spot a red glow coming from a tree. "There she is!" you call.

You find Ruby frozen in a tiny vial of ice. But a gentle touch from Saskia's wand sets the Red Fairy free!

"Thank you so much!" cries Ruby.

* If you decide to take Ruby straight back to Fairyland, go to 13.

* If you think it's safer to cast a spell, sending the goblins back to Jack Frost, go to 41.

While the greedy goblins scoff their doughnuts, you flutter along the shelves looking for a sign that Ruby may have been near.

"Goodness!" you suddenly whisper. "What's that?"

You realise that a bag of flour has tipped over onto the shelf! To your surprise, however, someone has traced a message in the powder with a tiny fairy finger.

The words say:

You wonder what the message might mean. While the goblins are busy filling their stomachs with the stolen cakes, you flutter bravely across the room.

"Whoever wrote that message sounds like they're in trouble," you decide. "It's up to me to help them!"

* If you decide to fly out through a gap in the window, go to 25.

* If you think the best escape route is out of the back door, go to 34.

"How can I ever thank you?" asks Ruby, thrilled to be free.

You smile modestly, then point up to the sky.

"Let's put the colour back into the human world," you suggest. "Then the Fairyland celebrations can begin!"

"Hurrah!" smiles Cherry. "I'll bring a batch of my yummiest cakes to the party later!"

You and Ruby flutter slowly over the towns and fields below. As you fly, colour streams out of Ruby's wand. Red traffic lights are returned, strawberry fields look scrummy again, and scarlet party dresses make a welcome return!

As you fly through a fluffy white cloud, Ruby leaves the last piece of magic to you.

"See that rainbow below us?" she beams. "Just touch it with your hand."

You reach down and touch its glossy surface, your fingers tingling with fairy magic. At once a red blaze appears at the top, glittering brightly in the afternoon sun!

The End

The goblin charges at you faster than your little
fairy wings can fly. Quickly, you hide in the
buggy, next to the baby.

The baby gurgles happily and waves her
rattle. Her mum steers the pushchair away into
Wetherbury Park. When it's safe, you peep out.
To your surprise, everyone in the park has a
glum face.

What's going on here? you wonder.

You blow the baby a kiss, then flutter out for
a closer look. Without the colour red, the flowers,
swings and slides aren't nearly as jolly as they used
to be. No one is smiling or laughing – in fact the
entire playground seems to be in a bad mood.

Z–z–zip!

Just then a flash of gold whizzes past you, faster
than a streak of light.

* If you decide to follow the strange gold light, go to 22.

* If you decide to stay where you are until you've discovered
  what's happening, go to 36.

You close your eyes and wish for a sign as to where Ruby might be. Could Jack Frost and his goblins have taken her back to the Ice Castle, or is she somewhere in the human world?

As you try to think, you are overcome by a funny, tickling sensation that makes you twitch your nose. You open your eyes to see Sienna darting above you, sprinkling pink fairy dust all around. The bedroom is lit up with thousands of stars that tingle as they touch your skin.

"What's happening?" you ask, watching the furniture suddenly grow bigger and bigger.

"I'm shrinking you down to fairy-size," smiles Sienna.

You smile in delight as two gauzy wings appear on your back. You manage to gently flap your wings backwards and forwards, until you find yourself fluttering up off the floor! You circle around your bedroom doing loop-the-loops.

"I can fly!" you shout, your voice tinkling in the same sweet way as Sienna's.

The Fun Day Fairy smiles then takes your hand. "Now you're ready to go and find Ruby!"

* If you decide to fly off towards Jack Frost's Ice Castle, go to 42.

* If you ask Sienna to lead you to the Fairyland Palace instead, go to 54.

You ask Sienna to take you to Fairyland straightaway. Even if Jack Frost and his goblins have smuggled Ruby out of the kingdom, they might have left a clue behind!

"Good idea!" smiles Sienna, spiralling up to the ceiling.

Suddenly your hair feels shimmery and tickly. You look up to see the Fun Day Fairy flying above you, sprinkling a fountain of fairy dust all around.

"What's happening?" you ask, as the room around you begins to grow bigger and bigger.

"I'm shrinking you down to fairy-size of course!" Sienna bursts into giggles, then points at the gauzy pair of wings that have appeared on your back.

Before you can say another word the wings begin to gently flap. It only takes a little wriggle of your shoulders to make them go faster. You walk to the end of the bed and look down – can you really be only a few centimetres tall?

"Ready to go?" asks your new friend, pointing to the bedroom window.

You reach for Sienna's hand and gently flutter out of the window and into the sky.

"Look!" you cry, after a little while. "I can see

my school!"

Sienna nods, then leads you further up, towards a row of white puffy clouds. You fly through the clouds for a long time.

"We're just above Fairyland now," Sienna says. "Where do you want to go first?"

* If you decide to seek out the Rainbow Fairies, go to 15.

* If you think it's best to visit King Oberon and Queen Titania at the Fairyland Palace, go to 46.

You flutter as fast as you can out of the back door, but the goblins have already spotted you.

"Come back here!" they bellow, pushing past each other to get to you.

As the pair chase you out of the yard, you dart into the shelter of a holly tree. The tree is covered with berries, but not a single one is its normal glistening ruby red colour.

"We'll get you now!" roars one of the goblins.

The daft creature reaches in to grab you, but the prickly leaves soon send him packing!

You sit on a branch catching your breath, until a little voice makes you jump with surprise.

"Thank goodness you've come!" says Holly the Christmas Fairy, fluttering up to sit next to you. Her red cape, dress and boots aren't nearly as jolly as normal, and you can guess why.

"We need Ruby to come back fast!" she sighs. "Things are desperate at Santa's cabin."

Holly's eyes fill with tears. She explains that if red is not restored again soon, there won't be any sparkle at Christmas this year.

"I won't let that happen!" you promise her.

You climb up the top of the tree. In the distance you see a tiny red dot, but you also see the goblins scurrying away!

* If you decide to flutter after the goblins, go to 12.

* If you decide to fly towards a tiny red dot that you can see twinkling in the distance, go to 24.

You curtsey to the king and queen, then follow them into the royal ballroom. It's a magnificent room, but something isn't right.

"See these drab velvet drapes?" whispers Sienna the Saturday Fairy. "They used to be a rich red, but they faded when Ruby was taken."

There's only one faint glow of red, coming from a footman carrying a silver platter. On the platter is a necklace carved in the shape of a rose.

"That's Ruby's necklace!" cries Sky.

The queen nods. "Jack Frost's magic wasn't quite strong enough to take this from the kingdom."

The pendant still has some of Ruby's magic, casting beautiful rosy beams on the windows all around.

The queen gently clasps the necklace around your neck. "Take this, dear friend," she says. "It will help you find Ruby."

"I'm afraid you need to go on your own," says Sienna sadly. "We must stay here and defend Fairyland. We can't risk Jack Frost stirring up more trouble."

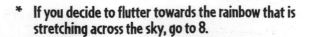

* If you decide to flutter towards the rainbow that is stretching across the sky, go to 8.

* If you think it's better to fly out over the toadstool houses that are dotting the hillsides, go to 39.

You flit curiously around the park, noticing that none of the children seem to want to talk to each other.

"What's that?" you suddenly gasp.

You've spotted a beautiful plumed bird perched on the fence. "What's the matter?" you ask. "Why are you sad?"

The magnificent creature stays silent. But just then, a fairy appears with shiny auburn hair.

"I'm Erin the Firebird Fairy," she says. "This is my firebird, Giggles. He has the power to bring humour to the human world," she explains, hugging the bird. "But his special red tail feathers have faded."

You click your fingers with excitement. "It's because Jack Frost has kidnapped Ruby the Red Fairy!"

Suddenly you realise why the playground is so quiet. People can't have fun without a laugh and a joke!

"I'll find Ruby," you declare. "Don't worry!"

You wave goodbye to Erin and Giggles, clutching the precious rose pendant to your heart.

"Please, Ruby," you whisper to the skies, "show me how to find you."

* If you decide to flutter towards the afternoon sun, go to 3.

* If you'd prefer to fly as high as you can above the park, go to 14.

You hold onto Ruby's rose necklace and wish for her six sisters to return.

In a few moments Amber, Saffron, Fern, Sky, Izzy and Heather are fluttering in front of you!

"We'll take care of the goblins!" shouts Saffron. "You look for Ruby."

As you flutter around you hear a tiny voice in the distance. You follow the sound to a thicket overgrown with ivy. There is Ruby, frozen to the spot by Jack Frost's most powerful magic!

"I'll get you out of there!" you cry, although you're not sure what to do next. Then you think of the necklace again. It's sparkling in a halo of stars.

"I'll press the rose against the ice!" you say. As you do this, Jack Frost's spell melts away.

Ruby sits up and stretches her delicate arms. "Thank you so much!"

You suddenly hear a furious shout echoing across the countryside.

"That's Jack Frost," smiles Ruby. "When he's *truly* mad, you can hear his roar all the way from the Ice Castle!"

* If you decide to use Ruby's magic to take everyone home to Fairyland, go to 6.

* If you'd rather get rid of Jack Frost's goblins, go to 47.

The yellow footprints swerve to the left along the lane, before dripping away next to a shiny silver car, parked neatly outside the village church.

There's just time to hide behind a bench before two young bridesmaids step out of the car and walk under the archway that leads to the church.

However, instead of looking radiant with happiness, the girls seem sad. When you spot their bouquets you understand why – the blooms have

large, velvety petals and jet-black centres, but they are a horrible shade of grey. The dull flowers don't go with the dresses at all.

You realise they must be poppies but their lovely rich red colour has completely drained away!

Jack Frost's spell must be even stronger than you thought. Oh, where is Ruby?

* If you choose to flutter up to take a closer look at the bouquets, go to 43.

* If you decide to slip into the church before anybody sees you, go to 50.

Soon you are circling above the toadstool villages of Fairyland. At that moment, the necklace in your hand begins to shimmer and glow, sending showers of little red stars twinkling into the skies ahead of you.

"It's telling me to fly on," you say out loud.

Before you know it, your wings are whisking you further and further onwards, until Fairyland becomes a tiny dot. When at last you feel weary you realise that you have reached the human world. Flying over the gardens and houses, roads and schools feels strange and very exciting.

When you next gaze down, two girls are waving up at you.

"Hi, up there," shouts one with blonde hair. "Please come and say hello!"

You glide down to the garden below, landing gently on top of a bird table.

"My name's Rachel Walker," says the blonde girl. "And this is my best friend, Kirsty Tate."

★ Turn to the next page! ★

"Hello!" says Kirsty. "Let's go somewhere where we can talk."

The girls smile and lead you to the bottom of Kirsty's garden.

"Where am I?" you ask shyly.

"You're in Wetherbury Village," says Rachel. "Are you a Rainbow Magic fairy?"

"Not really," you explain. "But I'm trying to find one."

You tell Kirsty and Rachel all about Ruby. The girls are both shocked and surprised – they've been friends with Ruby for ages!

Kirsty frowns and thinks hard. "Jack Frost is bound to have ordered his goblins to keep Ruby hidden. Find them and you'll know you're on the right track."

"Watch out for signs of trouble," nods Rachel. "Goblins can't help leaving a trail of chaos wherever they go."

You give each girl a hug – what great advice! Now it's time to press on with your search.

* If you decide to fly down the lane that winds beside Kirsty's house, go to 11.

* If you decide to take a flutter past the weather vane perched on her shed roof, go to 27.

You fly out of the hall, desperately trying to think of a plan to help Saskia and save Ruby. In the garden, you discover a blaze of scarlets, damsons and reds!

"I've sent Fairyland into a terrible spin," cackles a mean voice from behind a tree.

Slowly, you tiptoe forwards, until there in front of you is Jack Frost, clutching Ruby in his icy hands!

"Leave her alone!" you shout.

Without thinking, you hold up Ruby's necklace, dazzling the Ice Lord with its red sparkles.

"What is this?" he bellows. Jack Frost drops Ruby just as the goblins chase Saskia into the garden.

You flutter over to help Ruby as Jack Frost turns furiously to his goblins. "I told you to take care of any interfering fairies!"

"It's so lovely to see you again, Ruby," smiles Saskia.

"Thank you," beams the Red Fairy. "Now let's get away from Jack Frost and his goblins!"

* If you decide to flutter back to King Oberon and Queen Titania's palace, go to 23.

* If you'd prefer to cast a spell to take you to the Rainbow Fairies' house, go to 51.

"You are a true friend!" gushes Ruby, her rosy cheeks framing a warm smile.

The pretty fairy hugs you, then waves her wand three times – creating a fountain of scarlet stars.

"Come back, colour!" she commands. A whirl of red circles surrounds her in a ribbon of light.

"What about the goblins?" you ask.

Before you can say another word, the naughty henchmen are whirled up in a swirl of magic, vanishing with a *ping!* Their furious shouting gets quieter and quieter, before finally disappearing altogether.

"They've been sent back to Jack Frost's Ice Castle," giggles Saskia. "Hurrah for Ruby!"

"Now we should go," says Ruby, holding out her hand. "My sisters will be missing me."

You take a last look at your pearly fairy wings. It has been an amazing day.

"Fly safely," you smile. "Thank you for such a magical adventure."

Saskia and Ruby look at each other and grin.

"Please come with us," begs Saskia.

"We're going to have a Rainbow Magic celebration at the Fairyland Palace," Ruby explains. "And you're the guest of honour!"

The End

42

In no time at all, you and Sienna are fluttering among the fluffy clouds above your house. After flying for a long time, Sienna leads you down to a barren land of icy mountains and plains, where Jack Frost's Ice Castle lies.

Sienna sighs. "I can't see anyone at all. Jack Frost and his goblins must be making mischief somewhere else!"

Then you both see a red dot glinting in the snow. You swoop down and find a delicate red necklace set with a crystal rose!

Sienna's wings start to tremble. "That's Ruby's pendant. She must have lost it when Jack Frost took her from Fairyland."

"She doesn't seem to be here anymore," you sigh. "Shall we look somewhere else?"

"Bring the necklace with you," says Sienna. "It'll bring you luck."

"Aren't you coming too?" you ask.

The Saturday Fairy gives you a hug. "I'm needed back at the palace. Are you brave enough to search on your own?"

* If you decide to make your way to Fairyland, go to 2.

* If you'd rather fly towards a rainbow you have glimpsed in the distance, go to 55.

You flutter up to one of the bridesmaid's posies, then tuck yourself in among the flowers as she starts to walk towards the church. Suddenly a tiny face peeps out and smiles back at you – Pippa the Poppy Fairy!

"It's so lovely to see you!" she beams.

Pippa explains that without any red, all the stunning blooms for this wedding have faded horribly. Even the Poppy Fairy's own lovely dress has lost all of its colour.

"Have you seen any goblins?" you ask. "Kirsty and Rachel said that if there was trouble, they wouldn't be far away.

Pippa sighs and shakes her head. "No I haven't. And if Ruby isn't found soon, the poor bride is going be so disappointed."

"I won't give up until Ruby's safe," you say. "I promise!"

You squeeze the fairy's hand and put on your most cheerful smile. It's time to wriggle your way out of the posy and fly away.

"Thank you," grins Pippa, "and good luck!"

* If you decide to flutter upwards into the afternoon sun, go to 3.

* If you choose to set your sights on a tiny red dot that you've spotted in the distance, go to 24.

44

You push off from the window frame and give your wings a flutter. You're flying! Before long you're even somersaulting and loop-the-looping like a true Rainbow Magic fairy.

"You're a natural!" smiles Sienna.

Together, you fly to Fairyland. It's a magical land, dotted with toadstool houses. But you notice that instead of shiny red roofs, all the little houses are topped with dull grey. The only house with a tinge of red is the one that Sienna says is the home of the Rainbow Fairies.

Suddenly, you spot something twinkling in the grass. You flutter over and pick up a necklace.

"That's Ruby's rose charm!" gasps Sienna.

The pendant still has enough magic to create a lovely scarlet glow over the house and the garden.

"Perhaps this rose necklace will help us find Ruby," you say.

"Are you brave enough to find her on your own?" asks Sienna. "I must stay and protect Fairyland from Jack Frost's magic."

You take a deep breath and nod your head.

* If you decide to flutter towards the rainbow you can see stretching across the sky, go to 8.

* If you would rather circle above the toadstool village, go to 39.

45

You clutch Ruby's necklace, hoping it will give you courage. Then you dart through the swing door to the back of the shop. In the kitchen the two goblins are feasting on scones and cakes. Even though the jammy doughnuts have lost their red centres, the greedy things are shovelling them in one after another.

"You naughty creatures!" you can't help but blurt out. "That food belongs to the café!"

"Who said that?" One of the goblins looks up, jam still dribbling out of his mouth.

"It's another pesky fairy!" grunts the other one. He takes an angry swipe at you.

You duck out of the way and hide behind a bag of flour on a shelf, your heart racing.

"I am so pleased to see you!" says a tinkly voice.

It's Scarlett the Garnet Fairy!

"Normally I would use my gemstone magic to  shrink the goblins," she sighs. "But without the colour red, my spells don't work."

* **If you decide to see if Ruby's necklace can give you magical powers, go to 20.**

* **If you want to suggest working together to push the flour off the shelf, go to 26.**

"Would you take me to the Fairyland Palace?"
you ask. "The king and queen might know where
I should look first."

"Good idea!" says Sienna.

You fly after her, towards a green hill in the
distance. At the top of it you can just make out the
palace's four pink towers glinting in the sunlight.
As you get closer, Sienna points to a small window.

"Let's drop down through there," she suggests.

Landing is quite tricky for a first-time flyer.
With a little flutter and a bump, you find yourself
on the floor of the royal throne room!

"Let me give you a hand," says a sweet voice.

You look up to see Heather the Violet Fairy,
with Amber, Saffron, Fern, Sky and Izzy crowding
around.

"She's here, Your Majesties," says Sienna,
dropping to a curtsey in front of King Oberon
and Queen Titania.

"Hello," you say shyly, stepping towards the
Rainbow Fairies and Their Royal Highnesses.

King Oberon's face lights up with a kind smile.

"Thank you for coming," he replies.

The queen nods. "We need a special girl to help
us search the human world for Ruby."

* If you decide to follow the king and queen into the ballroom,
  go to 35.

* If you'd rather walk with the king into the Spells Library, go to 49.

47

You and Cherry gaze in wonder as the seven
Rainbow Fairies hold hands and form a magical
fairy ring.

"Goblins are lost, go back to Jack Frost!" chants
Ruby, her lovely red wings glittering in the
afternoon sun.

The goblins yelp and groan as they find their
hands linked together by Ruby's magic. The next
instant they have gone – transported back to their
furious master.

Ruby giggles and leads you over to a puddle.

"Look in here," she smiles, touching the water
with her wand.

The puddle clears to show
you the goblins landing with
a bump next to Jack Frost.
He is shouting at the
silly creatures and
shaking his fist
with rage.

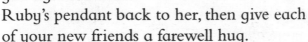

"It must be
time for me to
go home now,"
you sigh. You hand
Ruby's pendant back to her, then give each
of your new friends a farewell hug.

"Please visit us again soon," begs Heather the
Violet Fairy. "We'll have a party to celebrate!"

The Rainbow sisters stand around and cover
you with a multicoloured cascade of fairy dust –
and before you can blink you are back in your
bedroom again.

You look across and see a stunning rose petal
bracelet lying on your bed, with a label that reads:

Thank you for being the best fairy friend!
Ruby xx

The End

You flap your wings as fast as you can, using all your strength to fly over the goblin's head. The meanie tries to reach up and grasp you in his green, bony fingers, but he's just too slow!

"Drat!" shouts the goblin. "I'll get you for this!"

You keep on flying, not daring to turn around. You don't stop until you reach a tall slide in the middle of Wetherbury Park.

"Only…just…made it…" you pant, struggling to get your breath.

When you look up you notice that the playground is busy, but completely silent. All around you children are riding on roundabouts and being pushed on swings, but no one is laughing, smiling or even bothering to talk to each other.

"What's wrong?" you wonder out loud.

As you look from child to child, your eye is distracted by a flash of golden light. The beam circles over your head and then dives down behind a bush in front of you.

* If you decide to fly after the light, go to 22.

* If you choose to stay to see what has put all the children in a bad mood, go to 36.

King Oberon leads you all to the Spells Library —
a vast room lined from floor to ceiling with books.
Frog footmen, fairies and other palace folk work
quietly — some searching for spells, and others
writing in beautiful leather-bound books.

"I'd like to show you something," says the king.

He reaches up to a high shelf where one book
still glows in a rich shade of red. On top of the
book lies an exquisite pendant, carved in the shape
of a rose.

"That's Ruby's necklace!"
cries Fern the Green Fairy.
"She wears it every day."

The pendant casts a
beautiful red glow all
around the room.

"Jack Frost's powers weren't strong enough to
take Ruby *and* the necklace," the king explains. "If
you wear this on your quest, it will guide you
when you need help most."

"Aren't Sienna and the other fairies coming
with me?" you ask in surprise.

The king shakes his head. "I'm afraid they need
to stay and protect the kingdom from any further
wrongdoing. Good luck, my dear."

* **If you want to fly out towards Fairyland's toadstool villages, go to 39.**

* **If you decide to head for the rainbow you've spotted curving into the distance, go to 55.**

You swoop into the church and stop to take a breath in the cool, shady air. You look around for any goblins, but can't see any.

Just then there is a tiny tap on your shoulder. You jump round to see the friendly face of Pippa the Poppy Fairy!

"I'm so pleased you've come," she cries, her little dark eyes filling with tears. "This wedding is not going well at all!"

Pippa gives you a hug and explains that the bride had planned a wonderful wedding decorated with rich red poppies.

"But if Ruby isn't freed soon, the poor bride is going to be so disappointed!" the little fairy sighs.

You nod your head and wonder what to do next.

"I need to find the goblins," you decide. "I know they'll lead me to Ruby somehow."

"Let me try a spell," says Pippa, waving her wand. "Close your eyes," she says. "This should send you out of the church and on your way."

* If you discover when you open your eyes that you're whizzing upwards towards the golden sunshine, go to 3.

* If you find yourself floating high above the church steeple, go to 14.

Ruby waves her wand and you find you are in
the toadstool bedroom that she shares with the
Rainbow Fairies!

"I'm home!" calls Ruby happily.

Amber, Saffron, Fern, Sky, Izzy and Heather
flutter up the stairs.

"We're so glad you're back," beams Sky. "Now
Fairyland can be full of colour again!"

"The spell caused havoc in the human world
too," says Ruby. She looks at you and smiles.
"Thanks to you, I'm free and everything is back
to normal again."

"The king and queen are having a celebration
banquet to say thank you," Amber tells you.

Your heart glows with happiness. But you're
worried that your clothes aren't fit for a banquet!

"Don't worry, I'll lend you a gown to wear!"
smiles Ruby, opening a wardrobe full of party
frocks. "In red, of course!"

The End

You dart to the right after the yellow footprints, but before you can spot the goblin culprits, the paint runs out! Your retrace your steps and eventually find yourself outside the village church, quickly ducking behind an archway to avoid the throng of people streaming in.

"There must be a wedding today," you mutter. "Everyone looks very smart."

You carefully flutter over to a group of people gathered round two bridesmaids.

"These posies don't look right at all," says one of them, holding up a drab bouquet made of muddy pink flowers.

You can't help but agree. The two girls are wearing sweet dark-coloured dresses with layered net skirts, but their outfits don't seem to go with the posies at all.

"The bride asked for bunches of scarlet poppies," sighs the other one. "She's going to be so upset."

As the crowd shake their heads, and frown, you flutter silently above them. The flowers must be poppies that have lost all their stunning red colour! It makes you sad to think of the bride being disappointed on such a special day.

* If you decide to take a closer look at one of the posies, go to 43.

* If you think it's better to flutter inside the church to search for goblins, go to 50.

"I can fly!" you call out to Sienna.

You feel lighter than air as Sienna guides you through fluffy white clouds. Then you drop down into Fairyland.

But, without its rich cherry-red rooftops and scarlet flowers, Fairyland is not half as jolly as it ought to be.

"Look!" you suddenly cry, pointing to an object glittering on the ground below.

You both land gently in the grass, where you find a delicate red gem on a silvery chain.

"It's Ruby's rose pendant!" says Sienna. "I guess Ruby lost it when she was taken away."

The gem glows scarlet.

"The necklace must still have some magic," you say. "I'll wear it until I can return it to Ruby, its proper owner. Let's go, Sienna!"

But Sienna shakes her head. "While you search the human world, I must stay and defend Fairyland."

You give Sienna a hug, then look up to the sky, where you see a beautiful rainbow.

* **If you decide to flutter towards the pink turrets of the Fairyland Palace, go to 2.**

* **If you decide to set your sights on the rainbow curving over the skies above you, go to 8.**

You flutter your wings and gasp as you are transported up into the sky. Soon you are soaring above the pink turrets of the Fairyland Palace.

As soon as your feet touch down, the Rainbow Fairies rush up to give you a hug. Then they take you inside to meet King Oberon and Queen Titania.

The queen smiles gently. She gestures to the faded colours of the royal throne room, drained of its rich red furnishings.

"Thank you so much for coming. As you can see," she says, "we desperately need your help."

The king presents you with a delicate red necklace. It glows with a beautiful crimson light.

"This is Ruby's rose pendant," explains King Oberon. "It was found at the edge of Fairyland."

"Please take it," insists the queen. "Its magic will help you on your search."

"I am needed here to protect the palace," Sienna tells you.

"You mean I must go alone?" you ask, trembling at the thought.

* If you decide to fly towards the toadstool houses outside the palace, go to 39.

* If you choose to start your adventure by fluttering up towards the rainbow, go to 55.

You fly towards the rainbow that arches over the sky. It's beautiful, even without its bright band of red. Quickly, you jump on and slide down the rainbow all the way to the bottom.

It ends outside a pair of seaside cottages where two girls are in the garden painting seashells.

The blonde girls sees you straightaway. "Look, Kirsty," she says. "A new fairy. What's your name? I'm Rachel and this is my best friend, Kirsty."

The girls don't seem at all surprised to meet a fairy – in fact they tell you that they've been friends with the Rainbow Magic fairies for ages!

"The rainbow brought you back to the human world," says Kirsty. "This is Rainspell Island."

You tell the girls how Jack Frost has taken Ruby the Red Fairy.

"Poor Ruby!" cries Rachel. "Jack Frost and his goblins are such a nuisance!"

"Girls!" calls a voice. "Here's some lemonade."

"That's my mum!" whispers Rachel.

"I'd better go," you tell the girls. "It was so nice to meet you!"

* If you decide to fly away to explore the Island, go to 17.

* If you choose to head towards the sailboats twinkling in the harbour, go to 56.

You flutter towards the sailboats bobbing in the harbour, searching for a clue to where Ruby might be. You check all the boats, but there's nothing to suggest that there's magic nearby.

It's only when you decide to take a rest on the beach that something strange happens. Your thoughts are interrupted by a commotion from one of the seaside teashops.

"This is not good enough!" cries one voice.

"I demand my money back!" shrieks another.

You balance on the teashop sign, and peep in to see a crowd of angry people jostling and fighting inside. You notice that the shop is called the "Red Lobster", but the sign is painted in a muddy shade of brown. A closer look confirms what you've been thinking – all the red has disappeared from the teashop!

"The food doesn't look very nice at all," you sigh, feeling sorry for the café owner.

Strawberry jam with scones look faded and unappetising, while one lady's raspberry ice cream has turned a dull grey colour. A waiter turns round and carries a platter of doughnuts through to the back of the shop. It's then that you notice that the waiter is in fact a goblin, with big clumpy feet and an ugly green nose!

You sweep in and hide behind
a menu, carefully fluttering
from table to table until
you can spy on the goblin
out the back. In the
kitchen, the nasty creature
grins at another goblin friend.

The pair start scoffing from
the huge tray of doughnuts.

"I've found the goblins,"
you sigh. "Now where can
Ruby be?"

* If you decide to stay and eavesdrop on the goblins'
  conversation, go to 7.

* If you decide to go hunting for clues, go to 29.

Calling all Rainbow Magic fans

– the fairies need YOUR help!

Wicked Jack Frost has stolen

7 precious, glittering Jewel Fairy wands

and hidden them in 7 secret locations all over the countryside.

For your chance to WIN one of the 7 magical wands
AND to feature in a Rainbow Magic book
you must solve the clues in our Rainbow Magic Treasure Hunt!

To take part, all you have to do is:

1) Buy a copy of the special £1 Treasure Hunt edition of
Hannah the Happy Ever After Fairy (in shops from July 2009),
which contains a secret code.

2) Log on to **www.rainbowmagic.co.uk**, enter the special code
and select the region nearest to where you live.

3) Download your own special Rainbow Magic Treasure Map
and get your first Treasure Hunt clue telling you how to begin!

The first clue will be on the website on **Friday 3 July 2009**
and the Fun Day Fairies will be revealing a clue
every Friday for 7 weeks until **Friday 14 August 2009**,
when the last clue will be revealed.

Good Luck!